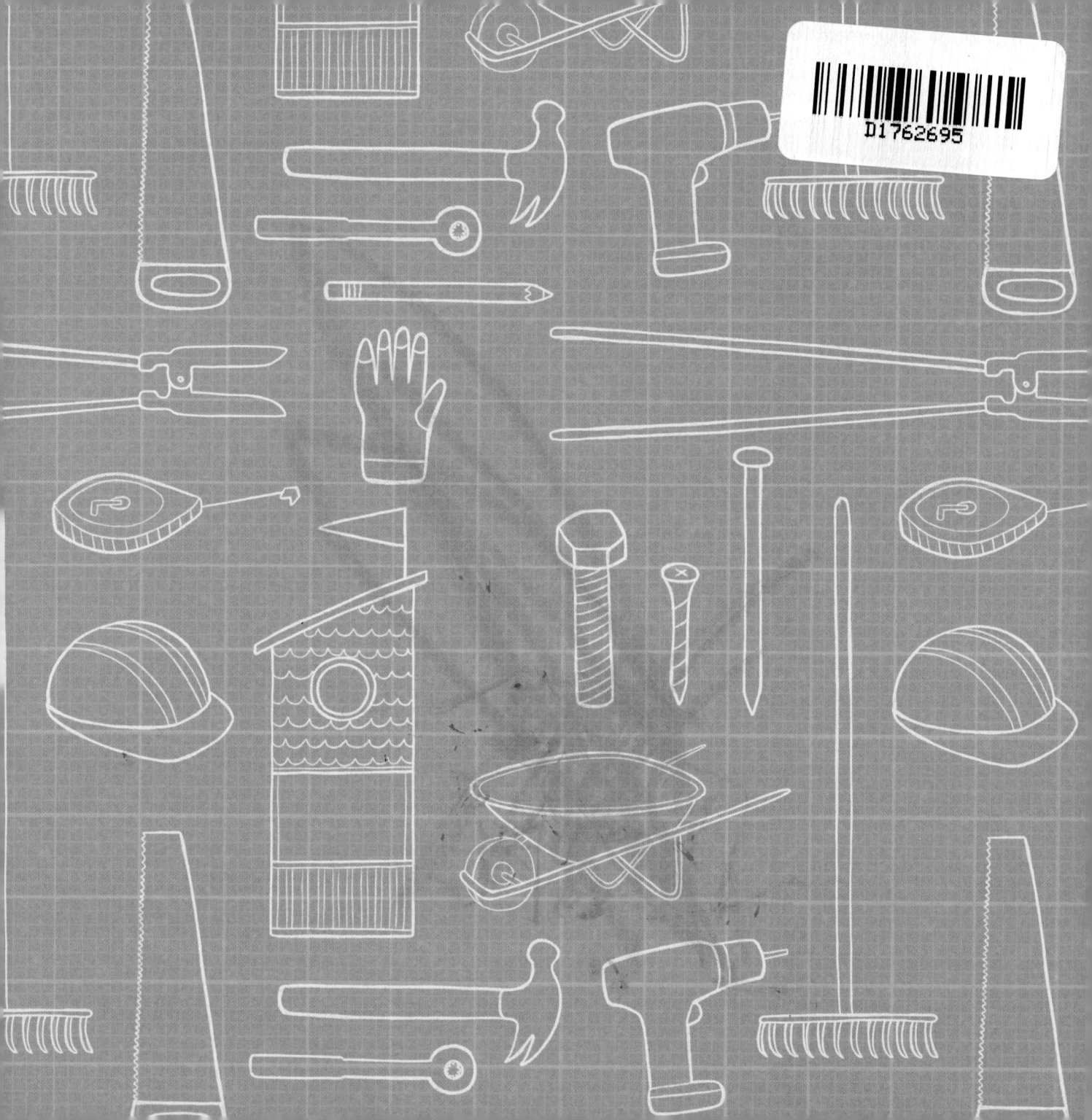

For my three DIY guys: Craig, Zach, and Lumpy—the supervisor.
—DA

To my dad: Thanks for showing me how to hammer nails
and how to build houses.
Love, Candice

Text copyright 2023 by Deb Adamson
Illustrations copyright 2023 by Candice Hartsough

All rights reserved.

Published by McSea Books   Lincoln, Maine
www.McSeaBooks.com

Manufactured by Regent Publishing Services Ltd. Printed in Shenzhen, China

No part of this publication may be reproduced, stored, or transmitted in any form
without written permission of the publisher.

Publisher's Cataloging-in-Publication Data

Names: Adamson, Deb, author. | Hartsough, Candice, illustrator.
Title: Bing, bang, pling / Deb Adamson ; Candice Hartsough, illustrator.
Description: Lincoln, ME : McSea Books, 2023. | Summary: A young girl helps her parents build a swing set. Names and sounds of tools used. | Audience: Pre-K to 2.
Identifiers: LCCN 2022923996 (print) | ISBN 978-1-954277-16-8 (hardcover)
Subjects: LCSH: Picture books for children. | CYAC: Tools--Fiction. | Play--Fiction. | Imagination--Fiction. | Stories in rhyme. | BISAC: JUVENILE FICTION / Imagination & Play. | JUVENILE FICTION / Family / General. | JUVENILE FICTION / Readers / Beginner. | JUVENILE FICTION / Stories in Verse.
Classification: LCC PZ7 .A33 Bi 2023 (print) | LCC PZ7 .A33 (ebook) | DDC [E]--dc23.

Printed in China

BING BANG PLING

By Deb Adamson
Illustrated by Candice Hartsough

So excited! Today's the day.

Supplies delivered in a heap.

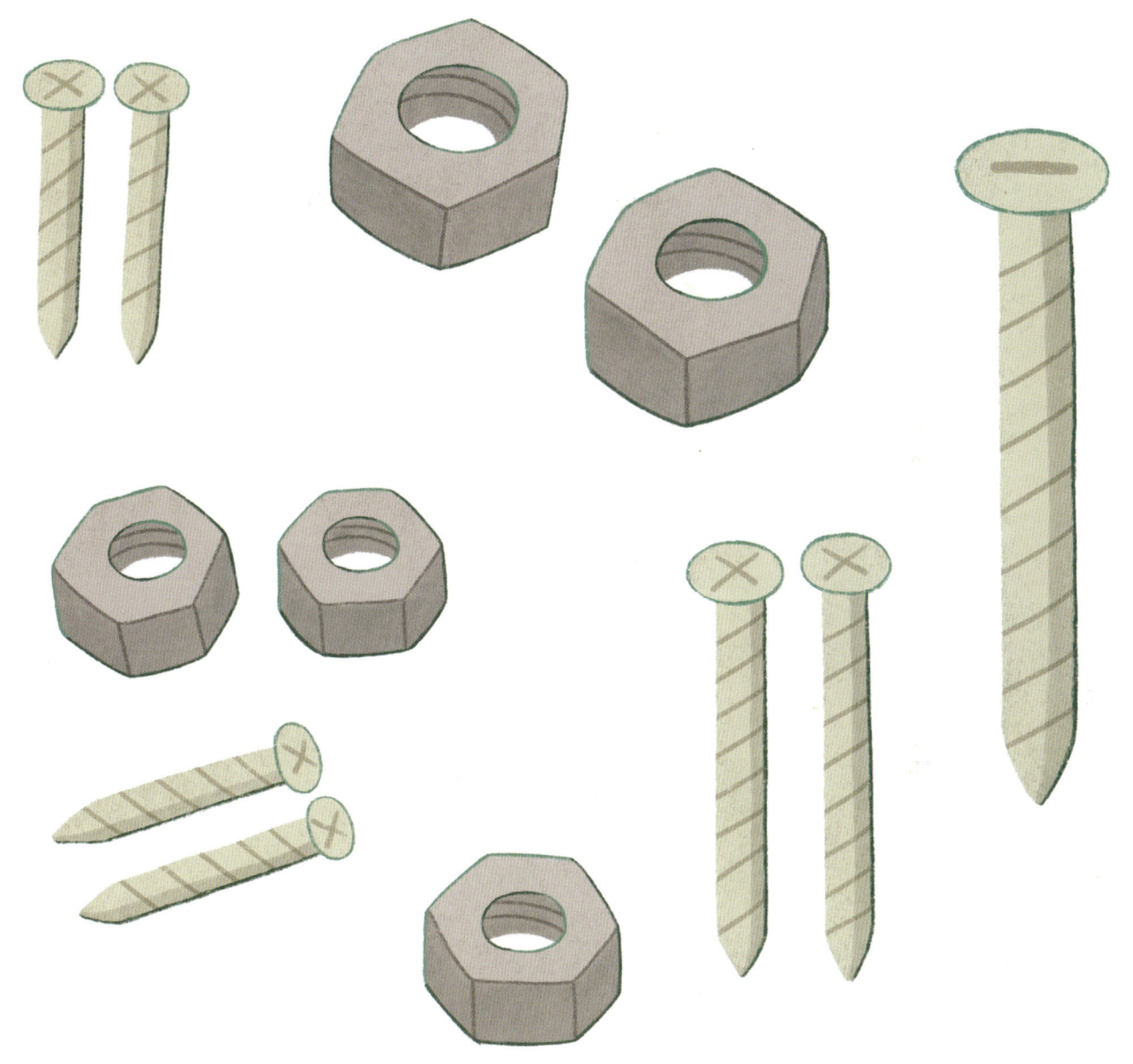

Count them out in ones and twos.

Mommy smooths some wood nearby,

"Get sandpaper. Now you try."

Daddy finishes with a *ZIP!*

Post-hole digger scooping dirt.

Daddy in a T-shirt.

Wheelbarrow, pour concrete.

Mommy whistles a happy sound.

Job is done. Tools away. Work has ended...

Now we play!

The End.

Deb Adamson lives on the Connecticut shoreline with her family, including orange cat extraordinaire, Fatty Lumpkin, aka Lumpy. Her books are silly, sweet, and often a combination of both. Visit her online at debadamson.com

Illustrator Candice Hartsough is inspired by relief printmaking, embroidery, and every pet or child she has ever met. She currently lives in Indianapolis, Indiana, with her husband, three children, and little dog. Visit her online at candiharts.com

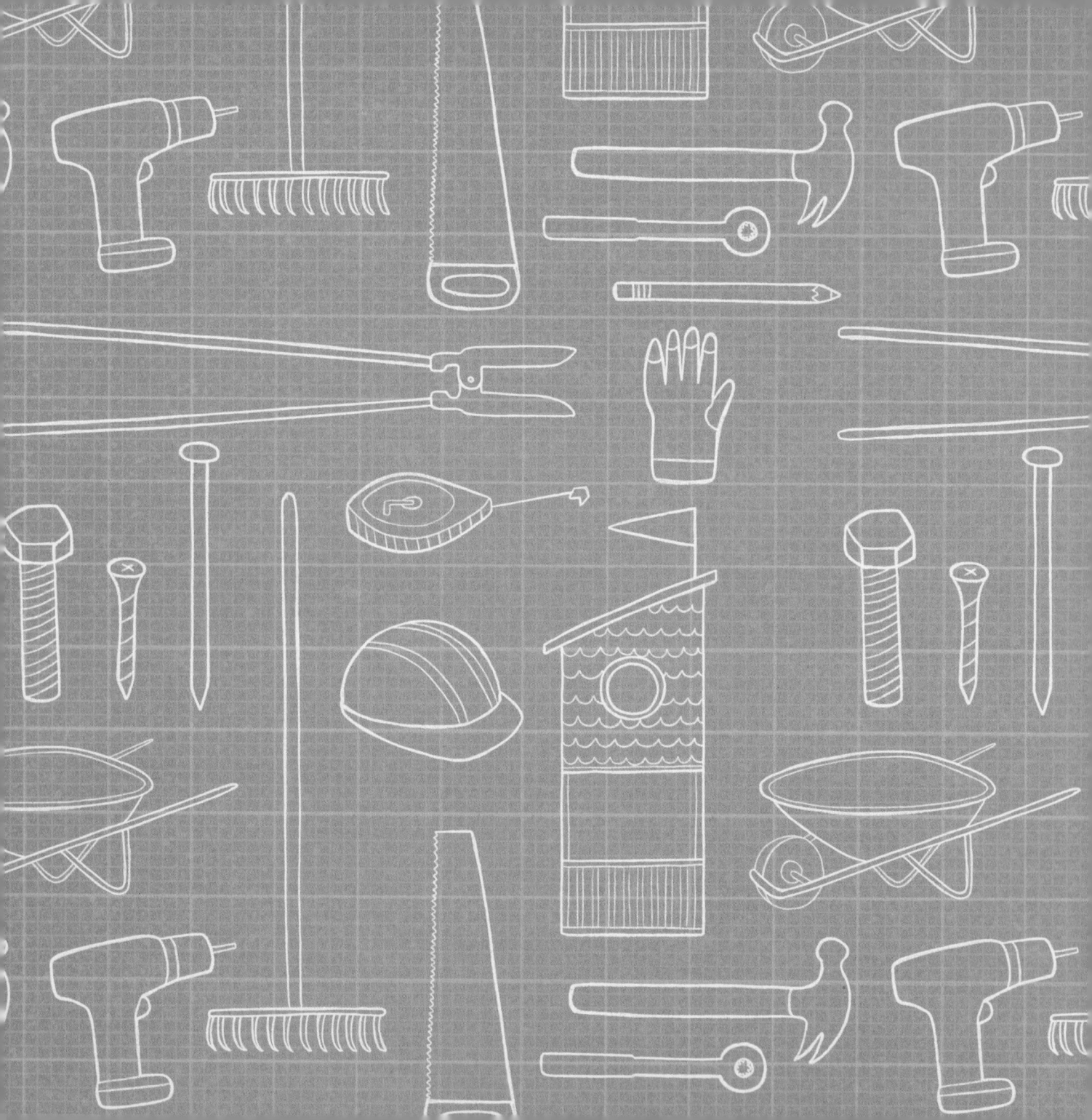